MW01059391

PICKPOCKET

Karen Spafford-Fitz

orca soundings

ORCA BOOK PUBLISHERS

Published in Canada and the United States in 2021 by Orca Book Publishers.
orcabook.com

Library and Archives Canada Cataloguing in Publication
Title: Pickpocket / Karen Spafford-Fitz.
Names: Spafford-Fitz, Karen, 1963– author.
Series: Orca soundings.
Description: Series statement: Orca soundings
Identifiers: Canadiana (print) 202002738973 |
Canadiana (ebook) 202002738981 |
ISBN 9781459827981 (softcover) | ISBN 9781459827998 (PDF) |
ISBN 9781459828001 (EPUB)
Classification: LCC PS8637.P33 P53 2021 | DDC jc813/.6—dc23

Library of Congress Control Number: 2020939248

Summary: In this high-interest accessible novel for teen readers,
seventeen-year-old Jean-Luc is sent away to live with his
uncle in a small town on the coast of France.

Orca Book Publishers is committed to reducing the consumption
of nonrenewable resources in the making of our books. We make
every effort to use materials that support a sustainable future.

Orca Book Publishers gratefully acknowledges the support for its
publishing programs provided by the following agencies: the Government
of Canada, the Canada Council for the Arts and the Province of British
Columbia through the BC Arts Council and the Book Publishing Tax Credit.

Edited by Tanya Trafford
Design by Ella Collier
Cover photography by Getty Images/Glowimages,
Getty Images/dangrytsku (front) and
Shutterstock.com/Krasovski Dmitri (back)

Printed and bound in Canada.

24 23 22 21 • 1 2 3 4

To Ken, Anna and Shannon—

my dearest travelers in Old Nice and in life.

Chapter One

I don't know if it's morning yet. And I don't know if I'm waking up or coming to. All I know is whatever I'm lying in smells disgusting!

Then it hits me like a punch to the gut. I'm lying in puke. It has dried into a gross, smelly crust on the side of my face and in my hair. I think it's just my puke, but I can't be sure.

I feel a stab of pain in my head as I shift on the carpet. I try to open my eyes. Nope—not happening.

"Catch you later!"

"See ya, Jean-Luc!"

I know those voices. My friends Owen and Tate.

A door slams, and the stabbing in my head intensifies. I pass out again. Next thing I know, someone is shaking my shoulder.

"Jean-Luc!" It's my dad.

I groan and slowly open one eye. I see beer cans, cigarette butts, crushed chips and other crap on the floor all around me.

I remember now. I told Owen and Tate my parents were going to be away.

"Let's have a little year-end party," Owen had said.

"Yeah," Tate had said. "An eleventh-grade blowout."

Before long, kids were streaming through the door. The music was pumping. The house was filled with beer kegs and tons of people. As for right now—

"Lève-toi!" Papa shakes me again. "Get up!"

I look up to see two people coming downstairs. The guy, Jonah—or maybe it's Jonas—is with a girl. I wish he'd zipped up his jeans before he left the bedroom. It's pretty obvious what they were just doing.

"Great party," he says. "See you around, Jean-Luc."

My dad drops a couple f-bombs. He usually swears in French. I guess he wanted to make sure Jonah/Jonas understood him too.

My mom is standing perfectly still—her overnight bag in her hand.

Papa turns to her. "Go grab the mop and bucket, Marie. And lots of cleaner."

Moments later my mom shoves the mop and bucket in front of me. Then a big bottle of pine cleaner.

"Start cleaning up this mess." Tears are forming in her eyes.

I reach for the bucket. Then I'm gagging and spitting out whatever was left in my stomach.

"Very impressive," Papa says. "Where are your fine friends now? I'm sure Tate and Otis had a part in trashing our home."

"Tate and Owen," I say.

"Whatever," Papa growls. "They'd be here helping you clean up if they were real friends."

I can't let him get away with that. "You don't know shit about my friends," I say.

Papa's face turns red. "They're not the great friends you think they are." He shakes his head. "You used to have nice, respectful friends."

He's talking about Anisha and Colin—my old friends. I needed to switch it up after my sister, Lena, died. But I can't go there.

"Use the garden hose to wash out that bucket," Papa says. "Then start cleaning up all this merde." All this shit.

Outside, the backyard spins and the sun stings my eyes. I hose out the bucket. The water is freezing cold.

Even so, I lean over and hose off my head too. Every drop of water feels like a razor cutting into my skin.

I pull out my phone to see if Tate and Owen have texted me. Nothing.

I take a closer look around the backyard. It's a mess out here too. I kick the beer cans into a pile. I straighten the table and chairs. I leave the squished flowers and cigarette butts for later.

I don't want to talk to Maman and Papa again, but I need to go back inside. Papa is in the kitchen.

"Do we have any Tylenol?" I ask.

"Check the shelf," he says. "The one with the door ripped off."

Oh man, he's right. I step over the cupboard door on the floor and reach for the bottle of pills. I swallow a couple with water. The whole time, my feet are sticking to the floor. I can't believe how much beer got spilled here last night. I also can't believe how much beer got drank.

Papa storms back out to the living room. He's talking to my mom now.

"La maison est un désastre!"

He's right. The house is definitely a disaster.

"Don't say that like it's my fault!" Maman says. "You know I don't like those friends of his any more than you do."

I clench the glass even tighter.

"I'm tempted to ring up Anisha and Colin," Papa says. "The way they ditched Jean-Luc after Lena took sick—"

Took sick. To hear him talk, you would think she'd had a sore throat, not leukemia. And now Papa wants to call Anisha and Colin? That's not going to happen!

"If anyone's to blame," Maman says, "it's you. You hardly spend any time here. You've made zero effort with your family lately."

I can't hear what Papa says next. But Maman

storms upstairs. Minutes later I hear a scream from their bedroom.

Papa races up the stairs. When he comes back down, his face is grim. "Volé," he says.

"Stolen?" I ask. "What was stolen?"

"Your mother's jewelry. Gone."

Oh no. Most of my mother's jewelry belonged to my grandmother. I often see my mom looking at it with a wistful expression on her face.

"Jean-Luc"—Papa stabs his finger toward me—"you will pay for everything that got broken or stolen." He heads back upstairs.

I pick up a few more plastic cups and food wrappers. I feel like I might be sick again. I need to sleep off this massive hangover.

I can hear my parents still arguing upstairs. It never used to be like this. But ever since Lena died, they can't agree on anything.

Screw this, I decide.

I flop down onto the couch. When I wake up, Maman and Papa are both standing over me.

"This can't go on," Maman says. "We can't deal with you constantly getting into trouble."

Papa nods. I can hardly believe it. It looks like my parents have finally agreed on something.

"So we have some news for you," Maman continues. "You're going to go work for your great-uncle Henri."

What? Who is Henri? I'm trying to make sense of this. "But I don't even know him!" is all I manage to say.

"That doesn't matter," Maman replied. "He has agreed to hire you to work at his shop for the summer. He has a large catering contract coming up."

"And you need the money," Papa says. "You will need to work all summer to earn enough to pay us back for all the damage."

"For the whole summer?" I'm still trying to clear my head. "Wait a minute. Is this the old guy who lives in France? Are you kidding? You're sending me to France?"

"Yes. To Nice—in the south, near the Mediterranean Sea," Maman says. I remember her talking about "Neese" and how she wishes she could go back. "It's beautiful there. This is a great opportunity. I think you're getting off lightly."

"I just bought your plane ticket online," Papa adds.

"You did what?" This is all happening too fast.

"You leave tomorrow morning." Maman rolls a suitcase toward me. "Start packing."

Chapter Two

The hangover lasts longer than the flight to Paris. I'm still sleeping it off during the second flight to Nice.

When the plane lands again, I check my phone. Still nothing from Tate and Owen. Just some messages from Maman.

When you leave the airport, hop on the bus to Old Nice. Then phone Henri.

Maman also texts me her uncle's phone number. I phone him as the bus pulls out.

"Allô?" The voice is old and gravelly.

"Hello. Er, allô. C'est moi—Jean-Luc." It's me.

I can't remember the last time I actually talked on the phone. The old man talks in a low voice, but I catch the name of my stop.

After about half an hour, I get off the bus and look around. My head clears for a moment. For the first time it starts to sink in that I am somewhere far from home.

"Jean-Luc?"

I turn. A man with white hair is standing there with a bike.

"Oui. Henri?" I ask.

He nods. "Bonsoir." Good evening.

It's definitely evening. The light is fading here. I'd lost track of time entirely. My brain is still fuzzy and sore.

Henri motions at me. I follow him as he pushes

his bike past a row of shops, then down a number of stone steps.

"Now we are in Old Nice," Henri says, sweeping his arm forward.

The word old seems exactly right. The damp, narrow streets look more like alleys. The whole place feels like a medieval village. All around us, people are bursting out of pubs and restaurants. Delicious food aromas waft through the air.

It's a slow walk. The streets are crowded, and I keep having to squeeze over to let motorcycles and scooters get past.

Suddenly Henri stops and points. "Et voilà. This is my shop," he says.

The sign above the door says Chez Rosa. Rosa's Place. Maman told me Rosa was Henri's wife. I never met her. She died a few years ago—not long after Lena died.

"This is where we make the socca," Henri says.

"Socca?" I ask.

Henri nods. "Tomorrow I will tell you all about it."

More people and motorcycles stream past us as we keep walking. After only a minute or two, Henri stops again. The heavy wooden door in front of us looks hundreds of years old.

"My apartment is upstairs."

We step inside the main area, and a faint light clicks on. The temperature has dropped a lot from what it was outside. I shiver in my light jacket, then follow Henri up a staircase. The stone steps are worn down in the middle. Every now and then I see a religious statue or a cross embedded in the walls.

Soon my legs are burning. But Henri is doing these steps like they're nothing, even though he's carrying his bike on his shoulder. He must be about seventy, and he's showing me up!

Finally Henri stops. He takes out an ancient key and opens a dark wooden door.

I roll my suitcase inside and look around. Henri's apartment is about the size of our living room back home. A couch and chair take up most of the main living space. The kitchen is just a small counter, a tiny sink and a set of burners to cook on. The fridge is smaller than my parents' bar fridge in the basement. I don't even see an oven. But at least he has a microwave. A table with two chairs is wedged up beside the counter.

I take another step inside. Now I can see that there's another room. Henri's bedroom maybe? And one more door just after it. I really hope it's a bathroom. And where am I supposed to sleep?

Henri steps forward and pulls a curtain back. A tiny cot is against the far wall. A small wooden table sits beside it.

That answers my question. This is my bedroom.

I wheel my suitcase up against the cot. I drop my backpack on top.

"You are hungry?" Henri asks.

"Oui," I say. I didn't eat much during the flights.

Henri pulls a baguette from a cupboard. He takes some cold cuts and cheese from the fridge.

He motions for me to sit down at the table. I start stuffing my face. I'm down to the last few pieces of meat when it hits me. Maybe Henri hasn't eaten dinner yet.

"Sorry," I say. "Is this for you too?"

Henri shakes his head. He doesn't seem to be a talker. That works for me.

When Henri had opened the cupboard, I saw just two or three plates and bowls. There's definitely no dishwasher. Once I've finished eating, I carry my dishes to the sink and wash them.

Henri finally speaks. "It's late," he says.

"What time is it?" I ask.

"Eight o'clock," he says.

That's late? Seriously?

"We start early to make the socca," Henri says. "So now, bedtime. After you tell your maman that you have arrived."

With a wave, Henri disappears behind the far door. I hear a flush. Thank god. It actually is a bathroom.

"Early start," Henri says again when he comes out. Then he goes into his bedroom and shuts the door behind him.

I lie on my cot with my eyes wide open. Sleep is the last thing on my mind. But I text my mom to say I've arrived safely at Henri's. Still nothing from Tate and Owen. It's early afternoon now back at home. They should be around. I wonder what they're doing.

Being halfway around the world from my friends totally sucks. I should have put up more of a fight when Maman and Papa said they were sending me here. I have a feeling this is going to be one long, boring summer.

Chapter Three

When I wake up, it takes me a few minutes to remember where I am. In Nice, France. On Henri's cot.

I check my phone for messages. Still nothing from my friends. Then I notice the time. Eleven o'clock. Shit!

I don't think this is what Henri meant when he said we would start early. I pull on blue jeans and a T-shirt.

"Henri?" I step out from behind my curtain.

Just as I suspected, he's not here. I tuck my phone and wallet into my pocket. Then I race out the apartment door. I only slow down on the stairs to pass an old woman walking up. I can see some tomatoes, a baguette and a paper package in her mesh bag.

When I get outside, the street is filled with dogs, motorcycles and lots of people. Some are speaking French and English. I don't recognize the other languages, except for some Arabic. My old friend Anisha used to speak it with her family.

Henri is outside his shop. He's craning his neck, looking down the street. Then he sees me.

"Sorry I'm late, Henri," I say. "I slept in. Jet lag, I think."

Henri nods. "That is okay for your first day," he says. "But only for your first day."

Just then a guy roars up to Chez Rosa on a motorcycle. I take another look at it. It's actually not a motorcycle. It's smaller than that. It's a Vespa—an

Italian scooter. It looks about a hundred years old. It's kind of cool. An open trailer is attached to it, with a large drum fastened inside.

The driver pulls to a stop and lifts off his helmet. "It broke down!" he says.

"Again, Marcel?" Henri asks.

"Oui." Marcel nods his head. "Right by the market. It took me twenty minutes to get it started again."

Henri throws his hands into the air. "Both of you, come load the socca."

I follow Henri into the shop. It feels like we just stepped into an oven.

Sure enough, a stone oven fills the back area. Wood is burning beneath the huge grill. Henri tosses me a set of oven mitts.

"For carrying the socca." He points to the round metal dishes filled with some kind of flatbread.

"Marcel." Henri turns to him. "Where are the trays from the market?"

Marcel turns and rushes from the shop.

"I have to tell him everything," Henri says, throwing up his hands. "He keeps my old Vespa running—most of the time. Otherwise I would fire him."

Marcel rushes back inside moments later. The empty trays clatter as he drops them onto the counter.

I pull on the mitts. Marcel and I carry trays of hot socca outside. We load them into the drum on top of the trailer.

Marcel is about to drive away when Henri stops him. "Take my nephew with you," he says. "Show Jean-Luc the market."

Marcel motions for me to get on the scooter behind him, and we take off. The street is getting busier all the time. Marcel sounds the horn when people don't move out of the way. He slows down when we come to an area with rows of tables near a tall stone wall. The tables are loaded down with fruits and vegetables, pastries and breads, honey, flowers and homemade soaps and lotions.

"Clara," Marcel says, turning off the engine. "More for you to sell."

An older woman with bright orange hair smiles.

"Very busy today," she says. "More tourists arriving every minute." Then she notices me. "Your helper is…"

"Jean-Luc, I think." Marcel shakes his head. "You know Henri. Working too hard to even introduce us."

"Hey, I'm Jean-Luc," I say. "I'm working for Henri this summer."

"And you just arrived from Canada, yes?" Clara asks.

"Yes," I say. "Last night."

Marcel opens the drum. He lifts out the trays of hot socca and lines them up on Clara's table.

Right away people appear—holding out money. Clara cuts the flatbread into strips and piles them onto pieces of waxed paper for the customers.

"This is socca?" I ask.

"Oui," Clara says. "You have never tried it?"

"No," I say.

Clara cuts a piece of socca for me. She watches while I take a bite. I've eaten lots of pancakes, as well as the thinner ones called crêpes. But socca is different from anything I've ever eaten. I stuff it into my mouth, savoring its creamy inside and crispy edges.

"You like it?" Clara asks, even though I'm sure she already knows the answer.

"Oui!" I say. "Oh my god, it's so good!"

Clara laughs. When there's a break in the crowd, she cuts me some more.

"We'd better get back." Marcel grabs the empty socca trays. "Henri will be waiting."

Marcel puts the lid back on the drum and fastens it. Soon we're weaving through the crowds on our way back to the shop.

Marcel and I do two more trips between Henri's shop and the market. When we pull up to the shop for the third time, Henri gives a nod.

Marcel pumps his fist into the air. "Another workday done!" he says.

Then he seems to notice the frown that has appeared on Henri's face.

"I just want to show Jean-Luc around town," Marcel says. "To make him feel at home."

"Fine," Henri says. "And tomorrow you will start on time. You know we cannot rush making the socca."

"Oui." Marcel nods. "Tomorrow will be a fresh, early day. We will make perfect socca."

Henri hands me a key. "The extra key to the apartment," he says. "You two can leave now. I will lock up."

As Marcel and I walk through town, he points out the main courtyards and popular gelato shops. The bustling cafés and patios where people are having drinks with their friends. The famous old churches. The castle on the hill.

"Have you worked for my uncle for long?" I ask.

"A year," Marcel says. "He's a good boss. But he forgets what it's like to be young. And to want to enjoy being with friends instead of always working."

I nod. Marcel could be talking about my parents.

Soon we're back by the market. The square is still busy. But the vendors have mostly shut down.

Marcel and I pass through the gates at the edge of Old Nice.

"The Mediterranean." Marcel points ahead as we cross the road. "The beach is down below. This part of the walkway is called the Promenade des Anglais—the Englishmen's Walk. People come from all over the world to walk here and enjoy our coast with its sparkling, blue water. And that blue, blue sky."

Marcel is right about the seawater and the sky. I take in all that blueness and then look around.

People are sunbathing, swimming and splashing at the shore. Others are farther out on paddleboards and kayaks.

Marcel points to the port. "Cruise ships take people up and down the coast. Monaco and Italy are very close."

"Cool," I say. "Maybe I'll check them out. But I don't think I'll ever figure out Old Nice. All those little streets are confusing."

"I will show you." Marcel checks the time. "This way," he says as he turns.

We soon come to a small dress shop. Marcel peers in the front window.

"Merde!" he says. "I'm late again."

"Late for what?" I ask.

"To see Yasmine," Marcel says. "She works here."

"Oh. Is Yasmine your girlfriend?"

"No." Marcel's face turns a faint red. "But soon, I hope."

He takes off his sunglasses and squints into the distance. "There she is! Up ahead!"

He starts to run down the street. Then he calls back to me, "See you tomorrow, Jean-Luc!"

With that he disappears into the crowd. I can't believe Marcel just ditched me! Where the hell am I anyway?

I'm cursing Marcel under my breath. I don't want to just stand here like a loser. So even though I have no idea how to get back to Henri's apartment, I start walking.

Chapter Four

These winding little streets make no sense to me.
Their names keep changing, even though I haven't
turned any corners. Gallo Street turns into Rossetti
Street. Droite Street turns into Gilly Street. I have to
dodge around people and motorcycles. I also realize
I'm starving.

I spot a gelato shop up ahead. I only have fifteen
euros in my wallet. That was all Maman had when

she shoved me on the plane. She said she'd transfer another hundred bucks to me. But it might take a few days before it shows up in my bank account. This is all the money I have until then.

My stomach gives another rumble. I veer over and join the lineup.

"Deux boules," I tell the man behind the gelato counter. Two scoops.

I'm walking and eating my gelato when I see the gates that lead out of the old city. At least I know where those take me.

I cross the road to the walkway along the sea. I'm checking out the girls on the beach below—especially the ones sunbathing with no tops on—and I'm about to go down for a closer look. Then I remember all the hours my sister and I used to spend along the waterfront back home.

Back home. Now I'm not thinking just about my sister. I'm wondering again why Owen and Tate haven't messaged me. Everyone at this beach is there with friends. They're laughing and talking and pulling snacks out of baskets and cloth bags. Going there by myself seems like a bad idea.

I'm turning away from the view when someone bumps into me. I jump, then I step back. I hadn't seen anyone there at all.

My first glance tells me this girl is about my age. And she's really pretty. Totally hot, actually.

My next glance tells me she's as surprised as I am. I'm a little awkward when it comes to talking to girls. I never know what to say. But this girl is looking at me with sparkling, dark eyes and a killer smile. It's time to speak up.

"Désolé," I say. "Sorry. I didn't see you there."

"Me either," she says. "I was looking down at the beach."

"Me too," I say.

Look at her face, Jean-Luc, not her boobs!

"Um, do you come here very often?" I ask. Then I nearly groan out loud. What a bad pickup line!

"Sometimes," she says.

Okay, at least she answered me. Maybe I didn't completely blow my chances with her.

"Are you going this way?" I ask.

For god's sake, Jean-Luc. Try that again!

"I mean, are you walking in my direction?" I ask.

"For a little while" she says. "I'm going to meet my family."

"Cool," I say. "My name is Jean-Luc, by the way."

"Selina," she says.

The last part of her name grabs my attention. I gasp.

"Something is wrong?" she asks.

"No," I say. "It's just...your name is a lot like my little sister's."

"Really?" Selina asks.

"Her name was Lena," I say. "She died a few years—"

What the hell has come over me? Why would I tell a total stranger something so heavy and so personal?

Selina looks back over her shoulder. I'm sure she'd rather talk to anyone but me. God, I'm such a loser! I need to save this situation if I can.

"Too bad I didn't bump into you earlier," I say. "I could have bought you a gelato." As I say that, I lift up the cup.

"Maybe next time." She smiles.

I like how she said that. Like she wants there to be a next time.

I can feel my mood shifting. If I can make something happen with Selina, maybe this summer will turn out okay after all.

We walk for a bit without talking. Then Selina announces, "I'm turning here."

"Oh. Well, see you later maybe," I say.

"I hope so," she says. "Have a good evening, Jean-Luc."

As she walks away, her blue dress sweeps around her butt and her legs. My eyes travel to her hand, clutching her leather bag.

Next time I'll be holding that hand! And from there, who knows?

I watch until she's out of sight. Then I turn back the way I came. I find Henri's street right away. Selina must be my good-luck charm!

I climb the cool, clammy steps up to Henri's apartment. I'm digging through my pockets for my key when I realize something. My wallet is missing!

I check all my pockets, but it's not there.

I think back to when I last had it. I took it out to pay the guy at the gelato place. But then I tucked it away in my back pocket. Didn't I?

I can't believe I lost my wallet on my second day here. I'm still checking my pockets as I make my way to my little curtained-off bedroom.

Then it hits me. I didn't lose my wallet. Someone stole it! Some jerk must have picked my pocket while I was out walking. I've heard thieves usually do that when the person is distracted. And I was totally distracted by the girls on the beach. By one in particular.

Selina!

Shit! I bet she stole my wallet. Just when I thought this summer was coming together. Those dreams I had about buying her gelato—and doing other stuff with her too—are all crumbling.

Then I remember something else. The picture in my wallet. The selfie I took of Lena and me hanging out along the waterfront. I took it just before Lena was diagnosed with leukemia. Back when we thought all the nosebleeds she was getting were no big deal.

I looked at that picture a lot after Lena died. And now it's gone. My heart is pounding so fast I can hardly hear Henri snoring in his bedroom. But sleep isn't going to happen for me. All I can think about is my missing wallet and that missing picture.

And about a cute, smiling pickpocket who chatted me up just long enough to trick me.

Just when I think my life can't suck any worse, it burns me. Over and over again.

Chapter Five

Someone is shaking me awake. What the hell?

I'm about to tell Papa to knock it off. Then I remember where I am.

"The socca." Henri's face is stern. "We start early today. Both of us."

Henri turns and steps back through the curtain. I want to tell him where he can shove his socca. I bite back the words, though, as I pull on some clothes.

Henri is washing dishes. I think he's already had breakfast. He pours something from a small white teapot into a cup. The smell of chocolate fills the air.

"Merci." I thank him as he hands me the hot chocolate.

Henri picks up some pastries from a plate. He tucks them into a thin paper sack.

"For you to eat later," he says. "While the socca rests."

While the socca *rests*? What the hell does that mean?

I follow Henri to the street. Only a few people are out this early. Up ahead a dog lifts its leg and takes a leak against the old building. Henri shoos it away, then unlocks the door of Chez Rosa.

The oven is already filled with pieces of wood. Henri shifts them around before he lights the fire. He fans it until the wood starts to burn.

Henri grabs a huge mixing bowl and opens a cupboard. A massive bag sits inside. He motions for me to slide it onto the counter.

"It's flour?" I ask.

"Oui," he says. "But not the wheat flour you use. This is chickpea flour."

"You can make flour out of chickpeas?" I ask.

Henri looks like he's about to answer me when Marcel skids into the shop.

"Late again!" Henri glares at him.

"Sorry," Marcel says, "but—"

"No excuses," Henri says. "I can't have this. Especially with the Exposition coming up."

"But Henri," Marcel says with a shrug, "that doesn't happen for weeks."

Henri's jaw tightens. "We must have our routines in place."

It seems like this Exposition is a big deal to Henri. Then I remember Maman mentioning that Henri has a big catering event coming up. Maybe that's what they're talking about.

"Go tend the fire, Marcel," Henri says.

While the shop heats up even more, I think about Marcel ditching me yesterday for his crush. If he hadn't done that, I wouldn't have been wandering along the promenade by myself. I'd probably still have my wallet.

"Pay attention, Jean-Luc," Henri says.

Shit! He's watching more closely than I thought.

"Add equal amounts of chickpea flour and water." He measures, then pours them into a large mixing bowl.

"Here. You stir." Henri hands me a wooden spoon.

When I have the flour and the water all mixed, Henri reaches for more ingredients.

"Next," he says, "olive oil and salt."

I keep stirring while he pours them in.

"Now we prepare the pans." Henri pours some olive oil into the first two. Then he hands me the jug of oil. He motions for me to oil the other pans.

Once I've done that, I turn to him. "What now?" I ask.

"Now the socca needs to rest," Henri says. "The water must absorb all the flour. So the texture of the socca will be creamy and rich."

Henri glances at the oven. "And the fire must be burning lower," he says. "While we wait, you two can eat. Outside." He shoos me toward the door.

I take the pastries Henri gave me earlier. As we pass through the shop, Marcel grabs two metal chairs. He carries them out front.

We sit down and Marcel gives me a sideways look. "Sorry I left you yesterday," he says.

I don't say anything right away. I'm not sure how pissed off to be with Marcel. I let him sweat while I pull out the pastries.

I finally turn to talk to him. "Did you ask her out?"

"Not yet." Marcel takes the second pastry from the bag. "But next time I will. What did you do after I left?"

I decide to stick it to him. "I got robbed," I say. "By a girl on the promenade."

"A pickpocket?" Marcel says.

"Oui. Now my wallet is gone. Stolen." I'm burning all over again just thinking about it. "That was my only cash," I say. "It wouldn't have happened except I got lost. I was an easy target."

I hadn't wanted to admit how helpless I was. But Marcel at least looks ashamed.

"Too bad," he says.

Henri calls us back into the shop. I watch him as he pours socca batter into the oiled pans and pops them into the oven.

"Marcel," Henri says, "go get the Vespa ready for market."

The store is soon filled with a delicious aroma. As soon as Henri pulls the hot trays out of the oven, we start loading them into the drum on the trailer. Just like the day before, I hop on behind Marcel.

When we get to the market, Clara waves us forward. Customers start lining up right away.

"I'm sorry about your stolen wallet," Marcel says once we've unloaded the socca. "Why don't you ask Henri for an advance on your pay?"

I highly doubt my mom's grumpy old uncle will go for that. I just shake my head and climb onto the scooter behind him.

When we get back to the shop, we do it all over again. We help Henri mix the batter. We add more wood to the fire. Then we deliver the next batch to Clara. We keep doing this until the market shuts down in late afternoon.

Henri is sending Marcel and me away. But first I have to ask him something. I have decided to take Marcel's advice after all.

"Henri, could you please give me some of my paycheck a little early?" I'm tripping over the words. I feel like I'm about eight years old.

Henri hesitates. I wonder how much Maman and Papa told him about the house party at our place.

"I wouldn't ask you," I say, "but I lost my wallet yesterday."

Marcel is biting his lip. Maybe he's wondering if I'm going to rat him out for ditching me.

Henri reaches into his wallet. He hands me a ten-euro note. "Be more careful with your wallet. There are lots of pickpockets in Old Nice. They look for tourists like you."

"I could have used that advice yesterday," I say, tucking the money away. "But thank you. Merci."

Chapter Six

It's hard to stay mad at Marcel. He's super easygoing. I'm also starting to think he might be the only friend I have. I've been in Nice for over a week now, and I still haven't heard from the guys back home.

Marcel is actually an okay friend. After work we hang out at the beach. We drink a little beer and wine. We watch his friends play beach volleyball. He still ditches me whenever he decides to go see

Yasmine. He insists every time that he's actually going to ask her out on a date. But every day he chickens out.

Henri, like always, does a crazy early bedtime. He pays us every Friday. Now that I've learned firsthand about pickpockets, I don't carry much money on me. I'm also enjoying spending time on my own.

Tonight I'm wandering along the promenade. I'm taking in the whole scene. The couples sharing food and drinks. Friends calling out to each other. Tourists stopping to read the signs. Then I see her. The girl who stole my wallet!

Selina is wearing the same blue dress. She's clutching the same leather purse. How many wallets does she have in there? Mine is probably long gone. Still—

"Arrête-toi!" I shout. Stop!

She looks back over her shoulder. Her face changes when she sees me. Next thing I know, she's racing across the walkway. I can't let her get away!

I start chasing her. I'm pumping my arms hard and running as fast as I can. When she veers over into the old town, I do the same.

I'm taking fast, tight breaths while I dodge cyclists and tourists in the market area. I bump into a couple as I shoot past the opera house café. I weave around all the bodies between me and her.

And now Selina is heading toward the trains. But when some people with cameras step in front of her, she has to slow down.

Yes! Just a few more steps and I'll catch her! I reach out and manage to get hold of her purse.

Selina starts shouting. "Policier!"

"Go ahead and scream for the police!" I say. "You can show them what's in your purse!"

All around us, people are staring. Selina is tugging on her purse. But I've got a good grip on it. And I'm not letting go.

Two police constables burst through the crowd. They're wearing camo shirts and pants. Handguns are strapped to their waists.

"What's going on here?" one of the officer asks.

"She stole my wallet." I gasp out the words. "Last week on the promenade."

Selina is shaking her head. She looks smaller and younger than the last time I saw her.

"I don't know what he is talking about," Selina says. "This man started chasing me when I was going to meet my parents."

"Where are your parents?" the officer asks.

"At the courtyard. They are having a glass of wine with my auntie."

"How old are you?" the other officer asks.

"Twelve."

Twelve? That can't be!

My mind flashes back to how I was planning to ask her out for gelato. Or to hang out at the beach. I thought she was sixteen or seventeen.

But she's twelve? That's the age my sister was when she died.

My whole body turns cold. My hand falls away from her purse.

"Did you steal this man's wallet?" the first officer asks her.

"No." Selina opens her purse wide. "I have just a few coins. I don't even have a wallet of my own," she says. "Papa says there are too many pickpockets in town."

The officer nods. "That is true," he says. When he looks at me, his eyes have hardened.

"What do you have to say for yourself?" he asks. "You were accosting a young person on the street. I need to see your ID."

"I don't have any ID," I say. "My wallet was stolen, remember?"

"Watch your tone. What is your name?" he asks.

"Jean-Luc Dupont. I got here nine days ago from Canada."

"Are you staying in Nice?"

"Oui. With my uncle," I say. "I'm working for him at Chez Rosa."

"I know that socca shop," the other officer says. "So if I go there next week, I will see you working there?"

"Yes, sir," I say.

The officer hesitates. "If you agree, young lady, we will perhaps let the young Canadian off with a warning this time."

All eyes turn to Selina. She shrinks beneath everyone's gaze. This is definitely not the vibe she was giving off last week!

"Oui." Selina nods. "But now I must go meet my parents. They will be worried about me."

"Of course," the officer says. "Go straight to your parents."

Selina closes her purse and hurries off.

The officer turns back to me. "I want no further disturbances from you."

"D'accord," I agree with them. I can't risk getting

into more trouble with no one here to back me up.

The officers turn and walk away. I look around, but Selina has disappeared into the crowd. A thought keeps running through my head. Twelve years old. She's just twelve years old.

That thought makes my stomach churn. It doesn't help that everyone is still staring at me. I need to get out of here.

I'm turning away when I notice a slip of paper on the ground. It must have fallen from Selina's purse when she left. I pick it up and have a look. It's a receipt from a place called Le Petit Monstre. The Little Monster. Maybe that's a kids' bookstore or something. I stuff it into my pocket and start walking back to Henri's apartment.

When I get there, Henri is poring over some papers in front of him.

"Bonsoir, Jean-Luc." Henri is pulling his little round glasses on and off. "This Exposition," he says. "So much to plan for."

"I'm sure you've thought of everything," I say.

"I hope so." He stands up. "But enough for tonight. I can't think about this anymore."

I nod. "I think I'm going to go to bed early too." I decide not to tell him about my run-in with the police.

Henri is still rattling around on the other side of the curtain. But silence quickly falls over the apartment.

I'm emptying out my pockets when I see the receipt Selina dropped. Le Petit Monstre. I wonder if it can help me track her down. Child or not, she did steal my wallet. I type the words into my phone.

But—hang on. It's a bar. And from what I see on their website, no twelve-year-old would be allowed to hang out there.

That can only mean one thing. Selina is a pickpocket and a liar.

As much as I want to set the record straight, I realize that things are going pretty well for me now. I think I need to put Selina out of my mind for good. She's already caused me more than enough trouble.

Chapter Seven

I'm finally figuring out Old Nice. The market, the opera house, the museum and the courthouse are great landmarks. They help me get back on track whenever I get lost. Of course, the best landmarks are the sea and the promenade that runs along the coast.

I'm also figuring out the socca. Henri has been hammering the method into me. About how to let the batter rest so the socca will have the right creamy texture. And about warming up the pans before cooking it. Henri doesn't trust Marcel to get the socca right. He threatens to fire Marcel at least once a week for being late. I don't think he really means it. I've heard him say more than once that the only reason he keeps Marcel around is for his mechanical skills. But I can tell he actually cares about him.

Today, like most days, the sun is beating down on Marcel and me as we take the socca to the market. Everywhere I look, there are people pushing carts or carrying cloth bags and baskets for their shopping.

As we get closer to Clara, some of the vendors wave to us. I know most of them by name now.

Manon, whose sun-warmed dates and apricots are crazy sweet.

Bruno with the loud voice, who calls out the price of his baked chickpeas every few minutes.

And Louis, who is carefully arranging his display of massive tomatoes. The sign says *Cœur de bœuf.*

Beef heart. The first time I read that, I thought he was selling real cows' hearts. We had to dissect those in Bio last year, and I nearly puked. Thank god this is just a type of tomato.

After Louis's table, it's Clara's. The small canopy at the far end protects her from the sun. It does nothing for the heat though. Clara's face is shiny red. She has completely sold out of socca.

Marcel swings the scooter over. I grab the empty trays from Clara. Marcel reaches into the large drum for the fresh trays of socca.

We deliver three more batches to Clara. Dripping with sweat, Marcel and I drop off the scooter at Chez Rosa. It's Friday, so Henri pays us and then waves us away.

"So what should we do tonight?" Marcel asks.

"Let's stop here," I say, pointing at the gelato place. It is still so hot outside.

"Gelato," Marcel says. "That's all I ever see you buy. What are you saving your money for?"

I'd rather not explain. I've been thinking about how I owe my parents more money than I can possibly make this summer. So I'm trying not to spend more than I have to. I don't hear from Maman and Papa very much. That probably means they're still pissed off at me. Considering all the stuff that got trashed or stolen at my party, that's fair.

Marcel still looks like he's waiting for an answer. I just shrug while we walk out onto the promenade.

Marcel points toward the beach. His friends Lola and Fabio are at the volleyball courts. "Let's go down there," he says.

"Hey, Marcel! Jean-Luc!" they call out as we join them on the smooth pebbles.

I've finished my gelato when Lola turns to me. "What do you think of Nice?" she asks.

"I'm getting used to it," I say. "It's way different from Canada."

"Because of how cold it gets there?" Fabio asks.

"Not just that," I say. "Lots of other things too. Like, here people take the time to sit and have a coffee or a glass of wine with their friends. Like, for no real reason."

"You need a reason?" Lola gives me a sideways look.

"I guess not," I say. "But in Canada, people mostly buy a drink and then they leave. They don't usually stay at the coffee shop and drink it there."

"So you just walk away?" Fabio asks. "And then you drink it?"

"Exactly," I say. "I've hardly ever finished a coffee at the coffee shop."

Fabio and Lola are shaking their heads.

"But that's why you buy a drink in the first place," Lola says. "To watch the people around you. Or to talk to your friends."

The conversation reminds me all over again that Tate and Owen still haven't messaged me. Not once since I've been here.

"So, Marcel," Fabio says. "Are you ever going to ask Yasmine out?"

"I think he will just keep torturing himself for another six months," Lola teases.

Marcel blushes. "I'm building up to it," he says. "Soon."

"I'll believe it when it happens," Fabio says, laughing.

We all leave the beach together. Fabio and Lola soon veer off the promenade. Marcel heads to the shop where Yasmine works.

I wander back through town on my own. I remember that the antique market is on tonight. Marcel had said it was worth checking out. Why not?

I follow the crowds, and when I get there, I can't believe the crazy mix of stuff for sale on dozens of long tables. Sheets of piano music. Brass door knockers in the shape of a hand. An old clarinet in a velvet-lined case. Heavy fur coats on yellow plastic hangers.

I stop when a necklace catches my eye. The copper pendant is in the shape of a star. It's hanging on a strand made of metal and sand-colored glass beads. It looks familiar to me.

It takes me a moment, but then I remember why. My mom used to have a necklace like this. She bought it at a street fair in San Francisco. The first time Tate and Owen came to our place, Maman was wearing it. She took off the necklace and set it down on the counter while she was making dinner. Later, she noticed it was gone.

I still remember how Maman's voice shook when she mentioned it to me.

"Is there any way your friends might have picked up the necklace?" she asked.

"They wouldn't have just 'picked it up,'" I said. "You think they stole it, don't you?"

Maman had hesitated. But now, standing in front of that table, I realize something. Owen and Tate did take the necklace. They used to laugh about stealing cigarettes from the corner store. They also stole a pair of expensive running shoes when a kid left his locker open at school.

My chest tightens when I remember what I did next. I yelled at my mom. Said she needed to leave my friends alone. I defended Owen and Tate, even though part of me had suspected even then that they had stolen it. Maman had finally run upstairs in tears.

And now my eyes are glued to the necklace in front of me. I need to talk to the vendor. I see a card on the table. His name is Gabri.

"Excusez-moi, monsieur."

Gabri's long gray ponytail flips over his shoulder as he turns. "Oui?" he asks.

"Le collier." I point to the necklace. "How much does it cost?"

Gabri hands me the necklace so I can look more closely at it. "Twenty-five euros," he says.

I was not expecting it to be so much. I don't have that on me. Maybe there's still a chance though. All around me, people are haggling with the vendors over prices. I need to do that too. I can't look too interested in the necklace or he'll charge me top price. I won't be able to afford it at all.

I shove the necklace back into his hand. "Too much," I say. "I'll find another one that isn't so expensive."

"But this necklace is very authentic," Gabri says. "You will not find anything of this quality for less than twenty-five euros."

I shake my head. I turn as though I'm going to leave.

"Perhaps," Gabri says, "I could sell it for twenty euros."

"Still too much," I say, taking a big risk.

"But such a quality piece," Gabri says.

I look around. The crowds are thinning.

"The market will soon close," I say. "I'll give you fifteen euros. Or you can pack up for the evening without selling it at all. Zero euros."

Gabri throws up his hands. "Okay," he says. "Fifteen euros!"

He slips the necklace into an envelope. "I hope your girlfriend likes it. Be sure to tell her you robbed an old man to buy it for her. Shameful." He shakes his head.

But I notice the hint of a smile on his face. I tuck the small package into my pocket. A warmth spreads through me when I think about giving it to Maman.

I'm still not ready to go back to the apartment. Instead, I walk up the hill toward the castle at the edge of town. I'm veering through the park when I come to a cemetery. Rows of elaborate tombstones stretch out in front of me.

I swallow hard. I didn't know there was a cemetery here. It brings back some terrible memories.

I'm turning away when I see someone standing near a crumbling monument.

Selina!

This time I won't let her get away. I have some questions I need answered.

Chapter Eight

Selina gasps when she sees me.

"I just want to talk," I say.

I don't know if she believes me. But at least she's not yelling for the cops this time.

"I know you stole my wallet," I say. "And I know you lied."

Plus, I kind of liked you the first time I met you.

Those words are running through my head too. But I know not to say them out loud.

"Lied?" Her voice shakes.

"You told the cops you were twelve. But no twelve-year-old would be hanging out at Le Petit Monstre."

Selina startles when I say the name of the bar.

"What do you know about that place?" Her voice shakes. Before I can answer, she adds, "I can't talk long. I have to meet someone."

"Your boyfriend?" I ask.

"Definitely not!" She flinches. She reaches up to push back her hair. The sleeve of her dress slides up. Her arm is covered in bruises and weird circular marks.

"Holy shit!" Before I can stop myself, I've reached for her wrist. "Who did this to you?"

She lets out a sob and pulls her arm away.

"What are those round marks?" I ask. "Not the bruises. The other ones."

Selina is tugging her sleeve down. She doesn't answer me. Then I realize what they are.

"Cigarette burns," I say.

A tear rolls down Selina's cheek. She nods. "Le Patron did it to me."

"Le Patron? You mean your boss?"

"Sort of. That's what everyone calls him."

My stomach clenches. "Where the hell do you work?"

Selina shakes her head. "I can't say," she says. "I don't have much time!"

"Tell me quickly," I say.

She takes a deep breath. "I couldn't live at home anymore," she says. "So I left to go live with my auntie. I was staying at a hostel while I figured out how to get to her place. One day a man started talking to me. He said he would give me a ride partway."

The knots in my stomach are growing tighter.

"But he brought me here. And now," Selina sobs, "he forces me to steal. Three hundred euros every day."

"So you pick people's pockets?"

"Yes. I must turn the money over to him. Or else—" Her voice catches in her throat.

"Or else he beats you," I say. "Or burns you."

"Yes." Her voice shakes. "Other things too."

I grit my teeth. I don't want to know what those other things might be.

"If you see me around town," she says, "do not talk to me. Le Patron will be watching." Her eyes are darting from side to side. "And I'm sorry about your wallet," she continues. "I didn't want to steal it. I had no choice."

She stands on her tiptoes and peers over the monument. "He's coming!" she says. "I have to go turn over my money to him."

As she brushes past me, I call out the question that's been nagging at me. "How old are you? Really?"

Selina pauses just long enough to answer. "Sixteen," she says. Then she dashes away.

Sixteen. Just like I thought. Still, my pulse races when I think about the nightmare Selina is living.

I need to keep walking. To burn off some steam.

As I circle the port, my mind is spinning. I can't stop thinking about Tate and Owen, who steal for fun. And about Selina, who is forced to steal—or else. Everything feels completely mixed up.

I finally head back to Henri's place. As usual, snoring is coming from Henri's bedroom. I need to get to sleep too. But images of Selina's bruises and cigarette burns keep me tossing and turning.

Then I remember the necklace I bought for my mom. It felt like the perfect gift for her. But maybe I should have given those fifteen euros to Selina instead. To try to keep her safe from Le Patron on those days when she hasn't made her full quota.

For the next few days, I go to all the places where I think pickpockets might hang out. The promenade.

The shopping center. The train station. The garden at the edge of town. I even go back to the cemetery. Each time, I take some money to slip to Selina or let her steal from my pocket. But I don't see her anywhere.

I can't give up though. And if I'm going to help her, I need to earn more money. So I start working extra hours. I don't even check with Henri first. I show up at the socca shop early. I also lock up after I've washed all the trays from the market.

Finally the end of the week rolls around. It's time to talk to Henri.

"Henri, I need to ask you something," I say. "It was great of you to let me have this summer job. I hope this isn't a problem. But I've been working some extra hours. So I wonder if you might give me—"

"A raise?" Henri finishes the sentence.

"Oui." I nod, heat spreading across my cheeks. "I need to earn a bit more."

Henri knows I need to pay back my parents for the house party. But I don't want to tell him I'm also setting aside money to help a girl. A girl I hardly know. A pickpocket. Someone I might never see again. So I don't go into details. Turns out, Henri doesn't need them.

He shrugs and then says, "You work more, you earn more. C'est tout." That's it.

Marcel is hovering nearby. I'm sure he hears us talking. When Henri steps away, Marcel leans over. "Are you trying to make me look bad, Jean-Luc?"

He looks so serious, I start to laugh.

"Relax, Marcel," I say. "One day you might even ask Yasmine out. Then I'll need some extra money to help you celebrate."

Marcel smiles widely. "One day I will do it," he says. "Maybe sooner than you think."

Somehow I doubt that. Then again, maybe Marcel will surprise me.

Chapter Nine

The next day I'm loading the first batch of socca into the trailer when I notice Marcel's long face.

"What's up?" I ask.

"I finally did it," he says.

"You asked Yasmine out? Really?"

"Well, I tried to," Marcel says. "I went to the shop where she works. Yasmine wasn't there. So I asked her manager about her." He heaves a sigh. "She told me

Yasmine left town. She moved to Lyon...with her new boyfriend."

"Oh no," I say. "That sucks, Marcel. But hey, you tried, right?"

"I guess," Marcel says. Then he fires up the Vespa and heads to the market.

While I mix the next batch of socca, I think back on all the places where I've looked for Selina. What if Le Patron has taken her out of the city? Or done something else to her?

Even with the heat from the wood oven, I shiver. I rack my brain about where else to look. Then I get an idea.

Le Petit Monstre. The bar that Selina had a receipt from.

It could be tricky for me to go there. Back home, I'm still too young to get into the bars. Someone always checks ID at the door. But everything seems more relaxed here in France. Still, I'm not brave enough to go to Le Petit Monstre by myself.

I wait until Marcel arrives back at the shop. When I ask him to go there with me, his eyes light up.

"There's a certain girl you want to meet there?" he asks.

I nod. "She sometimes hangs out there."

"This is good," Marcel says. "I struck out with Yasmine. But maybe this summer one of us will have a girlfriend after all."

Marcel's words stop me cold. A girlfriend? The situation with Selina is way more complicated than that. I need to help Selina for her own sake. And, in a weird way, for Lena's sake too. They both deserved a shot at having a decent life. And since my kid sister didn't get that, Selina needs it for sure. This feels like something I can get right for a change, especially after all the crap I pulled after Lena died.

Marcel is still looking at me. I think he's waiting for more details. But I don't know what Le Patron would do to Selina if he found out someone was trying to help her. I can't let this get out. The stakes are too high. And Marcel isn't the most reliable guy on the planet. So I keep it simple.

"Merci," I say.

"Tonight we will go to Le Petit Monstre," he says. "We will find your girl there."

I sure hope so, Marcel.

For the rest of the day, thoughts of going to the bar push everything else out of my head.

"Pay attention, Jean-Luc," Henri says with a frown. "You already added salt."

He's right. Plus, I keep forgetting how much flour I've put into the mixing bowl.

When Marcel returns with the empty trays, Henri turns to him.

"Take Jean-Luc to the market with you. His mind—oh là là." Henri shakes his head. "It is not on his work today."

I place the hot trays of socca into the drum. Henri goes back into the shop. A smile is playing across Marcel's face.

"That girl you like," Marcel says. "She must be très jolie. Very beautiful, yes?"

I grit my teeth.

"And I will be your—what is it called?" Marcel taps his forehead. Then he smiles. "I will be your wingman. I will tell all her friends what a great guy you are. And I will make sure you have time to talk to her by yourself."

Oh my god! Marcel is so off base!

Then again, I could use some time alone to talk to Selina. So I agree with his plan. Then I climb on behind him, and we take off to the market.

For the rest of the day, Henri hardly lets me back into the shop.

"The socca deserves better care," he says.

"D'accord, Henri," I say. "I'll pay better attention tomorrow."

"Non," Henri says. "You will not. Because tonight you are going to a bar with Marcel. I hear you boys talking. And tomorrow is a workday."

"I won't be late," I say.

Then again, the bars are open until well after midnight. What if Selina doesn't show up for hours?

"Actually, I might be a little late," I say.

"I know what happens when young men are out late having drinks at bars." Henri sighs. "Tomorrow morning you will be late for work. Just like Marcel. And you will make a mess of the socca. Too much salt. Not enough salt." He shakes his head.

I wish I could tell him what I'm doing. But I can't risk putting Selina in any more danger.

Over dinner, Henri is quieter than usual. My stomach is in knots. I can hardly eat the delicious chicken and vegetables in wine sauce that Henri has prepared. I am really starting to appreciate the food here. While he sops up the last of his supper with chunks of bread, I step over to the sink and start washing the dishes.

When I'm done, I take a quick shower. Then I grab some cash from my room and duck out the door.

"Au revoir, Henri!" I call. He just grunts.

Marcel is waiting for me on the promenade. Fabio and Lola are with him.

I turn to Marcel. "It's after seven thirty," I say. "We'd better get going."

"But the bar is just opening," Marcel says.

"It's way too early to go there." Fabio frowns at me.

"Let's hang out at the beach first," Lola says.

Seriously? Can we just get going?

I want to yell the words at them. But then I remind myself that these people know the bar scene better than I do. So when they head to the beach, I follow them.

Lola hands each of us small wine bottles from her bag. I take just a small drink of mine. I need a clear head tonight—if that's even possible. My mind is jumping all over the place. What if I've already missed Selina? Or what if she's not there?

I nudge Marcel.

"Dude!" he says, as some wine sloshes down his shirt. "What was that about?"

"Let's go," I say.

Marcel turns to Fabio and Lola. "You'll have to excuse Jean-Luc. He's all hot to go see this girl tonight. His mystery woman that he won't talk about."

"Really?" Lola sips her wine. "How did you meet her, Jean-Luc?"

I try to imagine how they'd react if I told them the truth.

I met her while she was picking my pocket. She's got a quick set of hands. That's such a turn-on!

"I'll tell you more after tonight," I say. "First I need to get my wingman moving."

Fabio gives Marcel a shove as he stands up.

"Bonne chance, Jean-Luc!" Lola says. Good luck!

We start walking. Soon the purple sign for Le Petit Monstre flashes ahead of us. I can see now that I didn't need to worry about not having ID. Because Selina is moving through the crowd outside the bar.

I know exactly what she's doing.

Chapter Ten

I want to run over and talk to Selina right away. But I can't let Marcel know who she is.

"Marcel," I say, "I need you to go inside for me."

"Really?" he says. "I can't be your wingman at a distance."

"But I need you to find out if they're checking ID," I say. "And to look for Selina for me."

"Ahh," Marcel says. "Your petite amie is named Selina."

Shit! I didn't mean to say her name! But right now I need Marcel out of here. Selina might take off!

"Oui." I try to keep my voice steady. "Her name is Selina. She has red, curly hair and blue eyes. She's almost as tall as I am. And she usually wears bright clothing."

I've just described the exact opposite of the petite, dark-haired Selina.

"Got it!" Marcel claps me on the shoulder. He slips into the crowd at the door.

I make my way over to Selina. I try to copy the easy smiles of the people around me.

"Selina." I say her name as quietly as I can. She turns toward me. My breath comes in a sharp gasp.

Selina looks more bruised and broken than she did just a week ago when I last saw her. More burns are visible down her arm. As the light from the sign pulses on and off, the dark hollows under her eyes almost glow. Her dress is hanging off her too. She's thinner than she used to be.

A moment later she seems to recognize me.

"I can't talk to you," she mutters. "I told you already. I'm working."

"I know," I say. "But—"

She interrupts me. "Le Patron has been extra hard on me lately. I made him angry."

I shake my head. "There's nothing you've done to deserve that." I motion toward her arms. Up close, I can also see a bruise forming on her forehead.

"I lost a receipt from here," she says. "Le Patron had sent me into the bar to get someone's phone number for him. So I chatted the guy up. Said I'd hook up with him later at his place. He wrote his number on the back of the receipt. But then I lost it before I could give it to Le Patron so…" Her voice trails off.

My knees shake beneath me.

"Wait!" I say. "You dropped a receipt that day at the train station. The day you called for the police. It fell out of your purse when you were leaving."

Selina leans in. "Was the receipt from this place?"

"Yes," I say. "I think I still have it. Meet me at the market tomorrow. I'll give it to you."

"That might help," Selina says. The exhaustion in her voice brings tears to my eyes. I blink hard.

She peers around at the crowd. "He can't see us talking," she says. "I can't risk angering him again."

"Pick my pocket," I say.

I turn. The pocket where I stashed the money is closest to her. I pretend I'm talking to two guys standing beside us.

Selina hesitates.

"Just do it," I mutter. "Hurry up!"

Selina gives me a bump. I can tell she has taken the money. From the corner of my eye, I see her slipping away.

I do a slow exhale. Then I start walking in the opposite direction from Selina.

"Jean-Luc!" Marcel calls out.

I turn around.

"I didn't see her," he says. "I asked all through the bar."

"It's okay," I say. "I saw Selina's best friend after you went inside." I tell him the story I prepared earlier. "She said Selina and her old boyfriend got back together. They're trying to work things out."

I hate lying to him. But I don't have any choice.

"Ah, women." Marcel slings an arm across my shoulder as we start walking. "We are not doing well with them these days. But maybe our luck will turn soon, hein?" he says.

"I hope so," I say. "The sooner, the better."

I wasn't out that late after all, but I didn't sleep well. Images of Selina wasting away kept streaming through my head. Images of my little sister wasting away in the hospital came next.

So the morning is a struggle. The only thing that gets me out of bed is my promise to Selina to get her the receipt. Just like yesterday, I can't keep anything straight at the socca shop.

"Jean-Luc," Henri says, "what is going on in your head? Again you forgot the salt. At this rate, I will have to train Marcel to make the socca. And that would be un désastre!"

It would definitely be a disaster if Marcel did the cooking. But today I can't seem to get my shit together.

"What to do with you..." Henri gives a long sigh. "And I worry about the Exposition coming up."

The Exposition. I've been so focused on helping Selina that I've hardly thought about Henri's big catering job. But Henri has been reviewing the number of guests. Planning the quantity of ingredients he needs. Figuring out when to start making the socca. Organizing how to get it there.

"That scooter," Henri says. "I hope I can count on it. Marcel can help somewhat. That boy has gasoline running through his veins. Still, there are breakdowns. Always breakdowns."

Just then, Marcel arrives with the empty trays. We load the fresh socca. Henri sends me back to the market with Marcel. I touch my pocket to be sure— even though I know I stashed the receipt and some extra cash there before I left the apartment this morning.

Marcel turns back to me. "I'm sorry things did not work out for you and Selina."

I need to just agree with him.

"Merci," I say. "I thought she was into me."

"I know what you mean," he says.

I kind of doubt it, Marcel. But whatever.

"Maybe we need to take a break from dating and girlfriends this summer," I say.

Marcel bursts out laughing. "You are joking, right?"

The whole time we're talking, I keep an eye out around me. I finally see Selina wandering through the market. Or pretending she's just wandering through the market.

While Marcel arranges the socca for Clara, I nudge him. "I'm going for a walk," I say. "I need to clear my head."

Marcel gives me a sympathetic smile. "I will cover for you," he says.

I make my way along the tables. The market is filled with tourists and locals doing their morning shop. I try to blend into the crowd as I approach Selina. I also try not to look directly at her. But I can't help it. I need to see how she's doing. If she has any fresh burns or bruises.

"Don't look at me," Selina mutters. "Le Patron has spies around town. Nobody can see us talking to each other."

"Back pocket," I say. I keep my eyes on the cut flowers in front of me as I speak.

"Merci."

I keep my face turned away from her. "Meet me at the cemetery on Friday," I say. "Seven o'clock."

I can't tell if she agrees or not. But I'll go there anyway. That'll be my chance to slip her some cash after I get paid—and see if she's still okay then.

When I'm sure she's left, I walk to the end of the market. Past the produce area and over to the flower vendors. For some reason, my thoughts turn to all the crappy things I've done since Lena died. To how hard I've been on my parents while they are dealing with their own sadness. And to how helping Selina feels like the right thing to do.

I'm by the gates that lead out onto the promenade when I realize something. Even though I'm giving Selina all the cash I can, it won't be enough. I'll go back to Canada. Le Patron will keep forcing Selina to rob people. And one day his anger will get the better of him. Then Selina will just disappear.

That thought haunts me. Giving her money is the only thing I can think of doing to help her right now. Maybe it will buy her some time.

But in the long run, it might not make any difference at all.

Chapter Eleven

For the next few weeks, I meet Selina whenever I can. I carry extra cash for her in my pocket. I try to make sure we're in a thick crowd of people. I keep changing our meeting spots, too, in case Le Patron or one of his spies is watching.

Today we're meeting by the flower vendors at the market. I haven't seen her yet. So while Marcel is tinkering with the Vespa, I wander over to buy a pastry.

I'm biting into it when I get an idea. Why didn't I think of this earlier? The answer seems so obvious.

Just then Selina bumps into me. Without looking at her, I say, "You know, we could call the police. They could deal with Le Patron."

Selina gasps. "Don't ever say that!" she says.

I turn to face her.

"Le Patron said if I ever call the police, I am dead within the day." Her eyes are wild with fear. "I will never get to my auntie's house in Toulouse."

I don't know what to say. I am out of ideas.

"We cannot meet again," she adds.

"What? Why not?"

"Le Patron saw me talking to you last time. He asked me who you were."

"What did you tell him?" I ask.

"That you are just a dumb tourist with lots of money in your pocket. And that I had to chat with you for a few minutes. Until I could pick your pocket."

Except for the part about me having lots of money, Selina is right. Because aside from giving her money from time to time, I feel dumber than ever. I don't know what to do.

I wander back toward Clara's table. I keep looking from side to side. Maybe one of the men around us is Le Patron.

I think about something Selina just said. Her aunt's house is in Toulouse. I've heard of that city before. I google it on my phone.

Toulouse is a five- to six-hour drive from Nice. To Selina, that must seem like a whole world away.

"Jean-Luc!" Marcel motions me over. "Henri will be waiting for us. Let's go!"

Marcel is right. Henri is pacing back and forth in front of Chez Rosa when we get there. With his big catering job coming up, he's been extra edgy.

"Hurry!" Henri says. "The socca is waiting."

He's hardly finished speaking when the Vespa sputters and cuts out.

"Broken down. Again!" Henri clenches his jaw.

I run inside and grab the tool kit. Marcel pulls out wrenches and screwdrivers and oil and other stuff. Tools are strewn across the stone path while he fixes and adjusts and tightens. Meanwhile I lift the empty socca trays from the back of the trailer.

I'm reaching deep into the drum when an idea hits me.

I know how to help Selina escape!

But to pull it off, I'll have to trust Marcel and Henri. And Selina will have to trust all of us.

I've seen how she trembles and how her face turns pale whenever she mentions Le Patron. But I think this plan could work. Still, gaining Selina's trust will be the toughest part of all.

I don't tell Henri and Marcel my plan right away. I just say that I have something important to discuss with them later. When we all gather in Henri's apartment, I close all the windows before I start to tell them about Selina being forced to rob people.

Henri keeps interrupting me. "That has been happening here?"

"Oui," I say. "Right here in Old Nice."

"In my city!" Henri's face is bright red. "We must help that young woman."

"How about the police?" Marcel asks.

"No police," I say. "Selina refuses. She won't last a minute if the police get involved. We need to help get her away from here as quickly and quietly as possible."

I pause to take a deep breath before I tell them the next part.

"The best time to help Selina escape is the night of the Exposition." I turn to my uncle. "I don't want to make that night more complicated, Henri. I know it's a big event for you. But there will be lots of diversions then. It's the perfect time to get Selina out of town without Le Patron noticing."

Henri doesn't say anything for a moment. "Then that is what we must do. We will get her away from that man. He is a blight on our city. In some ways, it is good my dear Rosa is not alive to hear of this."

"I know, Henri," I say. "I'm sorry."

Marcel leans forward in his chair. "What do you need me to do?"

"First of all, neither of you can tell anyone. If word gets out, Le Patron will hurt her even more. Or he'll take her somewhere else. Either way, she says she won't survive. And I believe her. I've seen what he's done to her. The bruises. The cigarette burns."

"Mon Dieu!" Marcel says. My god!

"Exactly," I say. "Le Patron has seen Selina and me talking. He's getting suspicious. So I'm going to meet with her just one more time. After that I need you to take over, Marcel. I need you to be Selina's messenger and driver."

"Anything," Marcel says. "I will do it."

"Thanks. To both of you," I say. "Here's what we need to do."

I describe the next steps. I even tell them that Selina's escape feels personal to me. That I care about Selina. That her well-being has somehow become tied to my little sister. And how helping Selina makes me feel like I'm making up for some stuff I'm not too proud of.

"I think my little sister would want me to do this," I say. "Thank you both for agreeing to help. The first thing I have to do is slip Selina a note telling her our plan."

I flop back into my chair. "But first I have to find her again."

Chapter Twelve

All week, I keep an eye out for Selina. I have the note in my pocket the whole time. But I don't see her anywhere. Not at the market, in the cemetery, along the promenade or at the shopping center.

I decide to check the train station. It was crazy busy when we met there before. I hope that also makes it the safest place for Selina. I just need to talk to her for a few seconds. Then I'll slip her the note that has the details about the escape plan.

While I hang around the train station, I try to think like a pickpocket. If I needed to rob people, where would I go?

Probably where people are distracted, while they're checking schedules and routes. And where they're pulling out their wallets to pay for their tickets.

I turn toward the ticket machines. Some police are strolling through the station. They're wearing guns and looking from side to side. I can't have them watching me or thinking I'm a person of interest.

But am I a person of interest now that I'm trying to help a pickpocket?

I take a deep breath. I try to do exactly what everyone else around me is doing. A guy standing next to me looks like he's around my age. When he moves closer to read the schedules, I do the same thing. And when he lines up to buy a ticket, so do I.

But Selina is still nowhere in sight. So when I get to the front, I pretend to take a phone call. I step out of the lineup.

While I walk back through the station, I pretend I'm checking the schedules again. I also scan the entire station. At the far end, some tourists are standing in a large group. They're wearing matching name tags around their necks. A tour guide is giving them instructions.

I scan the group. A small woman is weaving among them. My knees nearly give out when I see that it's Selina.

Deep breath, Jean-Luc.

I slowly make my way over to her. "Selina," I mutter. "I have a plan to get you away from here. To help you get to your aunt's place in Toulouse."

"What? What are you saying?" Selina hisses the words.

I look up at the schedule. *Don't make eye contact,* I remind myself.

"I have a plan. My uncle and my friend and me. We can help you escape."

From the corner of my eye, I see Selina shaking her head. "It's not possible," she says. "Le Patron will never—"

"I just hope you can trust us." I fix my eyes on the nearest ticket machine. "I absolutely believe we can do this."

Selina flits sideways. My heart nearly stops. She's running away—and I haven't given her the note yet!

I'm holding my breath until she weaves back toward me.

"I need to keep moving," she murmurs. "Le Patron is watching me more closely than ever. I gave him the receipt. Still..."

"Pick my pocket." I keep my face turned away. "The instructions are there. Plus some money."

"Le Patron knows who you are," Selina says. "It's dangerous talking to you at all."

"I'm sorry," I say. "This is the last time we'll talk. My friend Marcel—the guy I work with who drives the scooter—will drive you. You've seen Marcel, right?"

"Oui," Selina mutters.

"If you want to do this," I say, "Marcel will drive you partway to your aunt's house."

Selina turns toward some people behind us. The next thing I know, a brown leather wallet flashes. Selina slides it into the side pocket of her skirt. I'm sure nobody else noticed. I hardly saw her steal the wallet myself, and I was watching closely. Selina is one hell of a pickpocket!

"Take the note from my pocket," I say. "I hope you'll trust me. Everything is in the note."

"Why are you helping me?" she whispers.

I swallow hard.

"I've made some big mistakes," I mutter. "Especially after my sister died. I need to do something right for a change. And I want you to be safe."

When I turn back, she's gone. So are the note and the cash from my pocket. I think she heard me. And I hope she decides to trust me after all.

I'll know soon enough.

Chapter Thirteen

Assume that Le Patron is watching us all the time.

I've hammered those words into Marcel and Henri. We've also gone over the plan about a hundred times. There's a lot to think about. We need to make and deliver enough socca for everyone at the Exposition. And we need to time everything with Selina's escape.

Because the Exposition is happening tonight, we stopped delivering socca to the market earlier than usual. While I mix up more socca for tonight, I'm trying not to yawn. Last night I did a midnight drive in Fabio's truck. I left it near the Exposition. Then I took Henri's ancient bike from the back of the truck and cycled back to the apartment. I'm extra sleepy after all of that. Then again, I wouldn't have slept much anyway. I'm too wired about the plan.

Marcel has managed to get the scooter running better than ever. So I'm not at all surprised when the scooter putters and dies outside of the shop. Marcel made that happen right on cue.

Henri and I step out of the socca shop.

"Again that machine breaks down!" Henri shouts. "Tonight—when I have more socca than ever to deliver!"

I run forward to help Marcel push the scooter to the shop.

"Take it to the side!" Henri says. "Marcel, you must fix it. And do it right this time!"

We back the scooter into the alley beside Chez Rosa. With the trailer deep into the alley, I leave Marcel to work on it. I step back inside with Henri.

While the batter rests, all my worries about Selina rise to the surface—just like the bubbles in the socca batter. I still don't know if Selina is going to show up at all.

What if she's too afraid? What if she doesn't trust us? Or even worse, what if Le Patron has figured out that something is up?

But I can't think about everything that could go wrong. I need to make my best socca ever, like Henri taught me. The Exposition really matters to him. The whole time I work, I can feel his eyes on me.

Henri starts warming the pans. As always, it's blazing hot inside the shop. While the socca cooks, I pace around the shop, my shirt sticking to my sweaty body. I keep checking to see if the socca is done. Finally Henri gives me a nod.

Oh, thank god!

I burst through the crowd passing by the shop. At this time of day, many people are going for late-afternoon glasses of wine and beer.

"Marcel," I call, "the socca is ready. Have you fixed the scooter?"

Marcel is sprawled under the motor—a wrench in his hand. "Just finishing the last touches." He stands up and starts the engine.

Henri steps out of the shop. "Good work, Marcel," he says. "Jean-Luc will help you load the socca. Then you will drive to the Exposition—slowly, do you hear me? No revving the engine. That is why my poor Vespa keeps breaking down."

Marcel hangs his head. "Oui, Henri," he agrees.

I go back into the shop. I return holding trays of socca. I take the trays into the alley with Marcel.

"Open the drum for me," I tell him.

Marcel lifts the cover. It conceals us even more from the street. We exchange glances. In that moment, I can hardly breathe.

Then I hear a faint rustle deeper in the alley. I don't think anyone notices. But if they did, all they would see is a young boy wearing a cap, a jacket and a loose pair of pants.

While I help block the view from the street, the "young boy" slips into the drum. Then Marcel covers me while I tuck the socca trays into a crate I had shoved against the alley wall.

Marcel replaces the lid. We secure it to the drum with a cord. Then Marcel tugs his backpack onto his shoulders.

Courage. The word is on my lips as Marcel pulls away, towing the trailer behind him.

The minutes pass slower than ever as Henri and I finish making the socca for the Exposition. I pause when a vehicle pulls up outside the shop.

"Bonjour, Clara," Henri calls to her from the doorway. "Marcel has gone ahead to the Exposition. We have just the final batch of socca to load into your truck."

We carry tray after tray outside to Clara's truck. We ignore the people on the street who are struggling to squeeze past. Nobody seems to notice this final batch is larger than anyone might expect.

After we have it all loaded, Henri and I climb into the truck. Clara winds slowly through the narrow streets. She picks up speed once we leave Old Nice.

Henri is sitting next to me, his jaw set in a firm line. He wanted to tell Clara about Selina. But I reminded him that Selina is at greater risk if more people know. He finally agreed to wait.

Signs for the Exposition loom up ahead. As we pull into the hotel, I'm twitching in my seat. A man in a security uniform motions for us to stop.

Henri leans forward. "We have food for the Exposition," he says. "Socca from Chez Rosa. My assistant arrived earlier on a scooter."

Henri gives his name. The man motions us forward.

While Clara circles the hotel, I'm craning my neck. Sure enough, the scooter is sitting in the staff parking area. I'm desperate to talk to Marcel. But we won't see him for four more hours. That will give Marcel time to pick up Fabio's truck and drive Selina to Marseille—the next big city. From there, she'll take a train to her aunt's place in Toulouse. Marcel will drive back to us in Nice later tonight.

Clara is looking around. "Where is Marcel?" she asks.

I pretend I don't hear her. Before she can ask anything else, I dash to the back doors of the hotel. Inside, a tall woman with her hair in a tight bun is directing people around.

"Excuse me, madame," I say. "We have arrived with the socca."

The woman gives me a nod. Then she turns toward the people working in the kitchen. "We need carts," she says. "Vite!"

In an instant, people appear with carts. They wheel them to Clara's truck, then roll them back inside with the socca.

"Do you need me to stay and help?" Clara asks.

"No, merci," Henri says. "The Exposition has hired servers. I am here only if anyone wishes to learn more about socca. Or about my shop in Old Nice."

Clara nods. "Have a good evening, Henri. Everyone will love your socca," she says. "You have earned this honor tonight."

The whole time, I'm trying not to look at the clock. Instead, I watch as the staff place name cards and vases of flowers on the tables. They arrange the food for the buffet. Soon guests are streaming through the door.

But what's this? Marcel has just skidded into the room too! My heart nearly stops. I go and tug him out into the hallway.

"Marcel!" I say. "You're not supposed to be here yet! What happened?"

"She panicked." Marcel pauses to take a breath. "She kept saying he'd be looking for her."

Le Patron. "Tell me everything," I say.

"When we arrived here, I parked the Vespa between some cars so nobody could see her," Marcel continues. "I told her it was safer to come with me. That we could get away from Le Patron much faster. She finally got in Fabio's truck with me.

"I gave her the backpack with her next disguise and the money for her train ticket. After we passed Cannes, she asked me to stop for her to use a washroom. I waited and waited. But she didn't come back. I knew she had taken off."

I gasp. It feels like all the air just got knocked out of my lungs.

Henri joins us in the hallway. Marcel tells him what happened. Selina only made it an hour out of Nice with Marcel. My legs are shaking.

Henri lays a hand on my shoulder. "Your friend will be okay."

"You don't know that," I say.

"Not for certain," Henri says. "But she is a survivor. Also, she has money and a disguise."

I think back to last week at the train station. To how smoothly she lifted the man's wallet. Her pickpocket skills might help too.

All I can do now is hope she is still making her way to Toulouse.

Chapter Fourteen

With the Exposition behind us, Henri and I settle back into our old routine. We get up early. I help Henri make the socca. I go back and forth to the market. Then I hang out with Marcel.

I'm finishing the first batch of socca for today when Henri turns to me.

"You can take the rest of the day off," he says.

"Really?" I realize I've been so focused on making money for Selina that I haven't thought about taking a day off.

Marcel bursts into the shop minutes later.

"Jean-Luc is leaving work early," Henri tells him. "After this week, we will have to do without him. So this will be good practice."

"What will you do today?" Marcel asks me.

"I don't know," I say. "Any ideas?"

"You could explore the coast," Henri says. "Villefranche is beautiful."

Marcel nods. "And that beach...oh là là!"

"How do I get there?" I ask.

"Walk through the gates of Old Nice," Marcel says. "Then turn left and walk past the port. Follow the stone path along the sea. It will take you right there."

I grab my backpack from the apartment. Before I pass through the gates, I stop at the market.

"Jean-Luc," Clara calls. "Why aren't you working?"

"Henri gave me the day off."

"Bravo!" Clara says. "You have earned that!" She arranges an extra-large portion of socca on a piece of waxed paper.

As she hands it to me, she leans in. "Don't worry," she says. "Your petite amie will be fine."

My petite amie? She means Selina. But Selina isn't my girlfriend!

Still, I'm glad Henri told Clara the truth—even though Clara got some of the details wrong.

"Merci, Clara." I tuck the socca into my backpack. Next I buy sausage, cheese and a baguette. Then I start walking.

I pass the port, where the cruise ships are pulling in. Then I step onto the winding path. It's carved out of the jagged rocks above the sea. Benches and flat spaces have also been cut into them. People are lying there—the sun beating down on them as they talk and eat their picnic food.

While I walk, I think back to when I first came to Nice. I'd thought summer would drag on forever.

But next week I'm going home to Canada. I'll miss Henri and my new friends.

As for getting the money I need to pay back my parents, it hasn't happened. Other than buying the necklace for my mom, I gave most of what I earned to Selina. I'll probably need a part-time job while I finish high school.

When the path ends in front of me, I take the long staircase up to the street. I can soon see the beach up ahead. I walk for another ten minutes.

My mind soon turns back to Selina. When I was planning her escape, I didn't think about what would come after. About how tough it would be not knowing how she's doing. That will make it extra hard to leave Nice. I don't think I'll ever stop wondering if she's safe.

Just then a guy about my age nearly runs over me.

"Oh no! Désolé!" he cries as a frisbee clips me in the shoulder.

"No worries," I say. I toss the frisbee back to him.

"What a bad catch, Paul!" one of his friends calls.

Paul and his friends keep tossing the frisbee around. Every so often, they throw it to me too. They've drawn me into their group on this perfect little beach.

Their joking around takes me back to the days I spent with my old friends. To the kids I used to hang out with before Tate and Owen. I still remember what Papa said about Colin and Anisha.

I can't believe the way they ditched Jean-Luc after Lena took sick.

I didn't admit this to Papa or anyone else, but Colin and Anisha didn't ditch me. I just let my parents think that. It was easier than trying to explain what actually happened. That in those awful days after Lena died, I couldn't stand the sadness on their faces when they looked at me. They didn't know what to say to me. And I didn't know what I wanted them to say.

So I didn't answer their texts. I switched classes and completely avoided them. On those days when getting out of bed felt too heavy and sad to manage, that was all I could think to do. But now, with the laughter coming from the group around me, I'm thinking that wasn't the best idea.

Then I start to wonder something else. Whether maybe Tate and Owen actually did me a favor by ditching me this summer. I think they probably did.

With the frisbee soaring back and forth, I decide something. I'm going to get in touch with Colin and Anisha once I get home. It'll be awkward at first. But I'll tell them I'm sorry and that I was a jerk for ditching them after Lena died. I think they'll understand.

My new friend Paul drops the frisbee onto the beach. "I'm starving," he says.

All his buddies pull out some food and place it on a blanket. When they motion for me to join them, I add my stuff from the market. The socca is a bit soggy from being wrapped up. Everyone tells me it tastes amazing though. They smile extra widely when I tell them I helped make it.

Later, when everyone else packs up, I stand up to leave too.

"À la prochaine," Paul says. Till next time.

I wave, then start walking back to Old Nice. I follow the same winding trail along the sea—taking in the blue, blue sky and the salty air. After I pass through the gates to the old city, I go straight to Henri's apartment.

"Bonjour," I call from the door.

"Bonjour," Henri says. He hands me an envelope. "For you. This arrived in the mail today. It was sent to Chez Rosa."

I don't recognize the writing. But when I rip into the envelope, a photo slips out.

It's the picture of Lena and me. The photo from my wallet!

Selina must have sent this!

The photo looks more frayed and weathered than ever. I turn it over and see some writing on the back.

"Merci. Ça va bien." Thank you. All is well.

So she's okay. Selina is really okay. Suddenly a weight I didn't even know I was carrying lifts off my shoulders and chest. Tears stream down my face.

One thing is for sure. Selina did the hard work to make this happen. She took a chance on having a better life. She went for it. I am just glad I was able to give her a little nudge.

I realize Henri is staring at me, waiting to be filled in. I hand him the photo. He reads what's on the back of it. A smile covers his face.

"Bien. I have a question for you, Jean-Luc," Henri says. "I made an inquiry of an old friend here in Nice. A police officer who believes in this city, as I do. I asked Julien if he has heard of anyone forcing young people to become pickpockets.

"Julien had heard of this," Henri continues. "But the police have very little information. I said I might have some later. But that I first needed to know a certain young person was safe."

I realize what Henri is asking me. He wants me to tell the police about Le Patron. I know how fiercely proud Henri is of Old Nice. And I understand why. I have become very fond of this place too.

"Oui," I say.

I realize something else. It's time for me to make some changes. I need to do what Selina has done. I need to step forward into a new, better life. A life that includes friends who are actually friends.

And, hopefully, a life that includes more visits to Old Nice. To where the sun sparkles off the sea, and the sky is the bluest blue. And to where a young pickpocket helped me turn everything around—starting with the day she stole my wallet.

Acknowledgments

The first time I traveled to Old Nice, the apartment I rented was next to a socca shop called *Chez Thérésa*. Every day, Thérésa's family made the socca in the wood-burning oven, then transported it by scooter to the market. The mouth-watering flatbread won me over right away. The sparkling Mediterranean Sea, the charming markets and the winding streets also captured my imagination. I soon began dreaming of writing a story based around a socca shop in Old Nice.

Several years later, my editor at Orca—who clearly has a sixth sense about such things—asked me if I might like to write an adventure story set in France. I quickly agreed, even though I didn't yet have a full story in mind. Soon I was returning to Old Nice, though, inspired to dig more deeply into my earlier ideas.

Upon my arrival, various people warned me about pickpockets. I also did some research on child pickpocket rings operating elsewhere in France. Luckily for me, I returned to Canada with my wallet intact and my new story fully mapped out.

Thank you to the generous people of Old Nice who answered my questions over morning cappuccinos and afternoon glasses of rosé. Marc from *Marc de café* was especially helpful, as were his regular lunch patrons. Thérésa kindly offered me tips for making socca. My thanks as well to the friendly cab driver who explained the difference between driving motorcycles and scooters—like Henri's Vespa—throughout the old town.

A warm thank you to the entire Orca team for all that they do. Many thanks also to my family. Our shared time and love of Old Nice make every experience there even more joyful.

Special thanks to my husband, Ken, who snapped hundreds of research photos. His patience in tracing my characters' steps with me was truly heroic. Without him, I would still be hopelessly lost on those confusing, narrow streets...which, now that I think of it, sounds rather magical.

Karen Spafford-Fitz is the author of several novels for young people, including *Unity Club*, *Vanish* and *Dog Walker* in the Orca Currents line. She lives in Edmonton.